Clarion Books
a Houghton Mifflin Company imprint
215 Park Avenue South, New York, NY 10003

First published in the United Kingdom in 2003 by Oxford University Press. First American edition, 2004.

For information about permission to reproduce selections
from this book, write to Permissions, Houghton Mifflin Company,
215 Park Avenue South, New York, NY 10003.

www.houghtonmifflinbooks.com

Printed in Belgium.

Full cataloging information is available from the Library of Congress.

ISBN: 0-618-44397-5
LC#: 2003017805

10 9 8 7 6 5 4 3 2 1

To Elizabeth—J.E.

To David—A.R.

Someone Bigger

by Jonathan Emmett • Illustrated by Adrian Reynolds

Clarion Books
New York

Sam and Dad had made a kite.
They'd made it large.
They'd made it light.

They went out on a windy day
to see if they could fly it.

"Can I hold it first?" asked Sam.
"I'm old enough—I know I am!"
"No, you're too small!" his dad replied.
"*This* kite needs someone bigger."

Then Dad let go
        and launched the kite,

                        unwound

                        the string

                        and held it tight,

                        while Sam stood by

                        and watched,

                        and wished

                        that he was

                        someone bigger.

But the wind blew hard.
And the kite flew high.
And pulled Sam's dad *into the sky*.
And Sam went running after.

"Can I hold it now?" asked Sam.
"I'm old enough—I know I am!"
"No, you're too small!"
his father cried.
"This kite needs
someone bigger."

The kite flew up above the town,
where people tried to pull it down:

 a postman with a sack of mail,
a bank robber, escaped from jail . . .

. . . a policeman riding on a horse,
a bridegroom (and his bride, of course).

But *all* of them were pulled up, too!
And Sam went running after.

"Can I hold it now?"
asked Sam.
"I'm old enough—
I know I am!"
"No, you're too small!"
the people cried.
"This kitc needs
someone bigger."

And then, by some strange stroke of luck,
they flew right past a fire truck.

And when the firemen saw the kite,
they grabbed the string and held on tight.

But *all* of them were pulled up, too!
And Sam went running after.

"Can I hold it now?"
asked Sam.
"I'm old enough—
I know I am!"
"No, you're too small!"
the firemen cried.
"This kite needs
someone bigger."

The kite flew on—it would not fall.
It pulled a rhino from its stall . . .

. . . and other creatures from the zoo—
a tiger and a kangaroo!

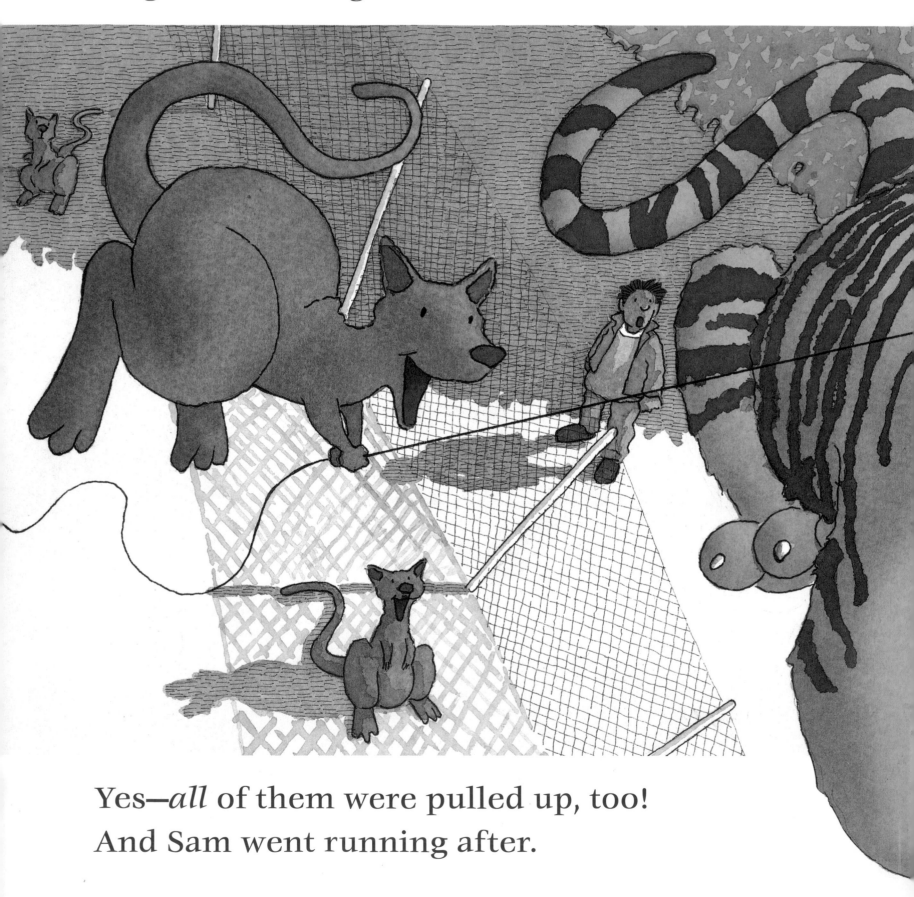

Yes—*all* of them were pulled up, too!
And Sam went running after.

"Can I hold it now?"
asked Sam.
"I'm old enough—
I know I am!"
"No, you're too small!"
the creatures cried.
"This kite needs
someone bigger."

But then Sam caught the kite—at last!
He grabbed the string and held it fast.
And even though he wound and wound,
his feet stayed firmly on the ground!

And, one by one, they came back down,
everyone from zoo and town:

postman, policeman, robber, horse,

rhino, tiger, kangaroo,
firemen, bride (and bridegroom, too),

and last of all, Sam's dad—of course!

"I'll hold it now," said Sam, "because
I'm old enough—I knew I was!
I'm not too small, and as you see,
this kite needs someone
JUST
LIKE
ME!"